Juana & Lucas
MUCHOS CHANGES

Juana & Lucas

MUCHOS CHANGES

Juana Medina

CANDLEWICK PRESS

All my gratitude to the best team I've had the pleasure of working with.
To Mary Lee Donovan, Melanie Córdova, Maryellen Hanley, Analía Cabello,
Phoebe Kosman—and everyone else at Candlewick Press who has dedicated
time and heart to help me find the right words to share the stories
of a Colombian girl and her beloved dog—thank you.

•   •   •

This is a work of fiction. Names, characters, places, and incidents are either
products of the author's imagination or, if real, are used fictitiously.

Copyright © 2021 by Juana Medina

First edition 2021

Library of Congress Catalog Card Number pending
ISBN 978-0-7636-7209-6

21 22 23 24 25 26 CCP 10 9 8 7 6 5 4 3 2 1

Printed in Shenzhen, Guangdong, China

This book was typeset in Nimrod and Avenir.
The illustrations were done in ink and watercolor.

Candlewick Press
99 Dover Street
Somerville, Massachusetts 02144

www.candlewick.com

A María, grande y fuerte

For Orson.
Welcome to this wild and beautiful world.

CHAPTER 1

My name is Juana. I live in Bogotá, Colombia, with my best *amigo*, Lucas. Not only is Lucas my most special friend, but he's also the best *perro* ever.

We live with my mami and with Luis. When Mami and Luis decided to get married, not everything was easy at first . . . but it has all worked out just fine. I'm okay with Mami marrying Luis. Why? *Porque* they love each other. Also, I get to listen to Luis's jazz collection and eat his special roasted Brussels sprouts whenever he makes them. I love *repollitas* (even more than cheese and ice cream). Lucas is also okay with us living all together in our new *casa*.

What I'm not that excited about is Mami's latest *sorpresa*: she is pregnant. This means there will soon be a baby in the house. Mami and Luis are VERY excited about this news, and they can't stop talking about it. Lucas and I, meanwhile, would much rather talk about other things. Like *fútbol* or *música*, or even the ever-changing Bogotá weather.

The thing I am very excited about is school break. For weeks, I won't have to worry about Mr. Tompkins. *¡HURRA!* Or about all the difficult math we're learning. Or about wearing my itchy uniform.

¡Bravo!

Woo-hoo!

During school breaks I rest, read, explore, and play with Lucas. Nothing is better than that. *¡Nada!* Perhaps we'll go swimming. And visit my *abuelos*. And go see Tía Cris and make some pottery together. I might even go on sleepovers with Cami and Pipe, like we've done so many times.

CHAPTER 2

It turns out, I got excited about my school break a little too soon. Mami had another *sorpresa* for me. She signed me up for skating camp.

A few weeks ago, I received a pair of skates as a gift from Luis and Mami. I was happy about them at first, but now, I'm a little less *feliz*.

I'd much rather have my feet on the ground than wobble and roll around on top of those weird *patines*. Adding wheels makes it much harder for me to stay upright.

Also, I don't know ANYONE going to skating camp. Mami says this will give me an *oportunidad* to make new friends, but I'm happy with the great *amigos* I already have.

Mami heard that Laura and Paula, our neighbors, who are already in high school, loved skating camp when they were little, and this makes her think I will love this, too. But Laura and Paula like a lot of things I do not like. NOT. ONE. BIT. Like makeup and dresses, and spending long afternoons doing nothing but watching TV and talking on their *teléfonos*.

"Juana, try skating at least five times," Mami said. I couldn't help but tell her, "Mami, there are things you don't have to try even once before you know you don't like them, like eating dirt or swimming with piranhas."

Mami agrees that neither of those things are worth trying even once, but in the case of skating camp, she's said there will be no debate and that that's the end of this *discusión*. So I guess I'll have to skate at least five times.

My skates are weird.
MUY. WEIRD.
This is why:

They came in a box with a strange-looking wrench to make the skates adjust to my feet. Luis and Mami told me having skates that grow is a good thing, because I will get to enjoy them for a long time.

The skates came all the way from Sweden, and the *instrucciones* are written in Swedish. Since I do not speak any Swedish, not even one bit, it is impossible for me to understand a single word.

The skates have nuts and
bolts all over the place.

They are metallic with yellow straps and orange wheels.
Strangely, shoes are strapped on to the skates.

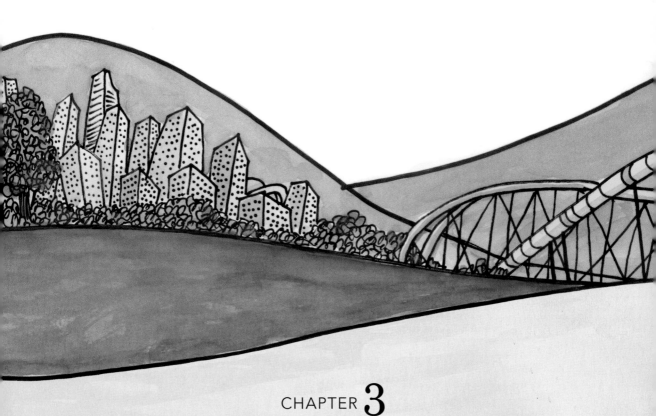

CHAPTER 3

The air feels fresh and the sun is bright.
Normally I would think that it's a beautiful morning.
But it's my first day of skating camp, and I don't feel all
that sunny.

Camp is in a huge park called Cuchavira. Mami drives
a long way through the park until we make it to the
parking lot.

Cuchavira is
enorme!

Cuchavira is an amazing park.
AMAZING!
And this is why:

There are swimming pools and water slides.
People who are braver than I am have
said they're pretty thrilling.

It has roller coasters and a Ferris wheel so big that it
can be seen from far away! When riding it, you can
see the Andes Mountains and beautiful sunsets.

There's a plane in the park. A REAL airplane!
This one doesn't fly anymore, but it can be used
to pretend-fly and to imagine great trips.

All sorts of camps take place here: karate, dancing, cycling, swimming,
golf, fencing. So many *opciones*, I can't remember all of them.

A large forest connects all sorts of sports fields. It's like
many parks in one big park. It feels as if it goes on forever!

Mami and I make our way through the park and finally arrive at skating camp. I see many people already skating, and they're all really good at it! Some are doing pirouettes and others are playing hockey. I surely can't do any of those things. I feel like disappearing into thin air.

Fortunately, I quickly learn that there are different levels. Some kids, just like me, don't know much beyond the fact that skates are for skating.

Not one other kid in *patinaje* camp has skates like mine. Their skates are all in the shape of boots, and they put them on over their socks.

CHAPTER 4

My level has *dos* coaches: Anita and Francisco. They seem very cheerful about skating, and they give us a whole show on how they can loop, jump, and race. Thankfully, they don't expect us to do all of that right away! First, they give each of us a large upside-down bucket we can hold on to and push as we skate up and down the rink.

The buckets make an awful lot of noise. We sound like a battalion of very loud hornets. After an hour of this, we are instructed to stand by the wall on one side of the rink and to let go of our buckets. Then Francisco glides as smoothly as butter on warm toast to the opposite side of the rink and stops. Anita tells us that, according to the *colores* of the wheels on our skates, we'll take turns skating over to Francisco.

"*¡AZUL!*" she calls. A large group of kids wearing blue-wheeled skates starts making its way toward Francisco. "*¡VERDE!*" Another bunch makes its move forward. "*¡AMARILLO!*" Onward goes another set of skaters. I wait by the wall, our group getting smaller and smaller. Finally, I hear Anita say, "*¡NARANJA! . . .* Okay, Juana, your turn."

Being the only one in skating camp with orange wheels is NOT. FUN. *Nada de* fun. I have to make my way across the rink all by myself. It makes my stomach twist when all eyes are on me.

I try my best, but my skate hits a pebble
on the ground. I lose my balance and

fly forward

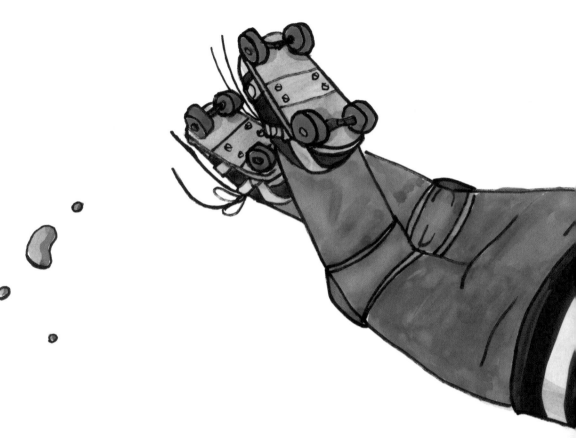

Now I'm not just the only one with different skates, but
the only one with a scraped chin and bruised elbow.

Thankfully, Anita skates to the rescue and helps me up, and we skate over to the other side of the rink. Francisco asks two *niñas* to get some *agua* while he runs to get the first aid kit.

Everyone gathers around to watch Francisco and Anita clean my chin and bandage it. These coaches are not only great at skating—they are really good people, too!

They tell the group it is a good time to take a break. I'm grateful for some time off my rolling feet.

During break, Andrea shares her crackers with me, Cata offers me a clementine, and Camilo is happy to trade his yogurt for some of my carrot sticks. It turns out, everyone was scared about falling and thinks I took the stumble like a pro. The fall was far from a good thing, but it showed me that maybe Mami was right—there might be room in my life for new *amigos*.

CHAPTER 5

That afternoon, Luis comes to pick me up
from skating camp. It's not what I was expecting, but I'll
still be able to tell Mami about my day.

When I get home, Mami has something to tell me. It turns out the baby growing inside Mami made a little hole in the sack that keeps it safe while it's growing.

Now Mami needs to stay very still so that the hole doesn't get any bigger and so that the baby can keep growing. Learning that Mami has to stay so still makes me sad. This baby hasn't even been born yet and it's already causing trouble!

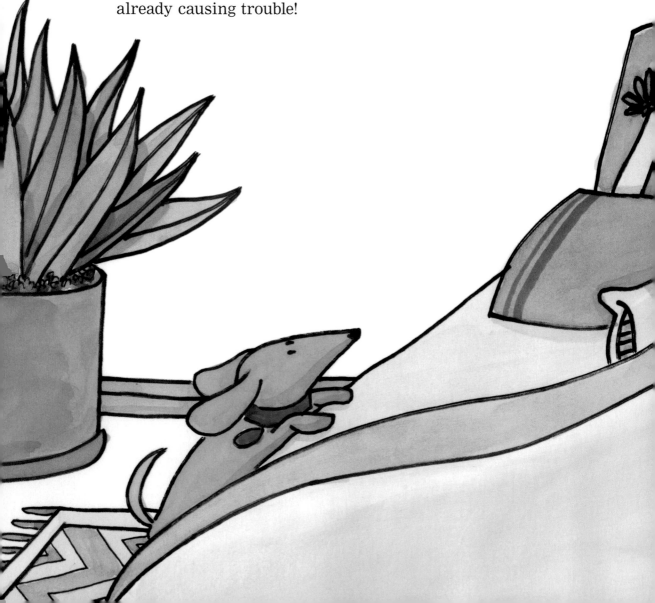

At least Mami is *muy feliz* to hear about my good day at camp, aside from the scraped chin, of course.

CHAPTER 6

The next day at skating camp, Cata, Andrea, and Camilo are waiting to hear how I'm feeling after yesterday's big skating *accidente*.

I tell my new friends about Mami being pregnant and about her having to stay in bed until the baby comes. We sit under a big magnolia tree to have our snack, and they listen to my horror story. Then they share some of their own.

It turns out Cata and Camilo are both older siblings and know a lot about babies. A. LOT.

Andrea is not an older sibling, but she is surrounded by **babies**: her cousins are twin **babies,** and her neighbor just had a L^{OUD} crying baby less than five months ago.

Babies make everything complicado. EVERYTHING!

And here's why:

Babies can't walk, so other people have to carry them EVERYWHERE.

They cry. TOO. MUCH.

Adults forget how to speak around them. It's all just awwws and ooohs. I fear grown-ups might melt into puddles just looking at babies.

They eat ALL. THE. TIME. Even in the middle of the night they have to wake up the whole family because they want to eat.

They are bald and wrinkly. Who ever thought babies were cute?

They can't speak or play or even read.

All the attention goes to these tiny *humanos*.

They don't clean up after themselves. They leave a big *desastre* behind them at all times!

After listening to my friends talk about everything that's wrong with *bebés*, I'm less worried about Mami being stuck in bed and more worried about this baby causing **major *dificultades*** for all!

CHAPTER 7

Perhaps one good thing about Mami having to stay in bed all the time is that I have been spending a lot of extra time with my *abuelos*. They have been picking me up after skating camp and taking me to their *casa*.

I LOVE my *abuelos'* house. And I love my *abuelos* even more than I love their house. Abuelita always has fresh *fruta* for me to eat after school, and Abuelo shares his delicious chocolates with me.

Abuelo, whom I call Abue (because it's shorter), has shown me books in his library that have pictures that show exactly how babies grow before they are even born. It seems like a **very complicated** thing, but he has very patiently explained to me how nicely the human body works.

He knows a lot about the human body because he is a doctor. Abue is a neurosurgeon, which is a complicated way of saying that he is a doctor who knows *MUCHÍSIMO* about the human brain. Because the brain is connected to

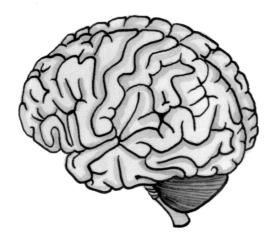

the rest of the body, he also knows a lot about the human body . . . and about tiny babies.

More importantly, he knows about being an older sibling. He says it isn't too bad to be one.

My *abuela* when she was little

Abuelita is the youngest of nine siblings, so she knows what it is like to be the baby in the family. I know that each one of her brothers and sisters loves her very much, so I guess she couldn't have been a bad baby. I can't imagine her being a bad baby. She is very *responsable*.

Abuelita and Abue think I will be a fantastic older sister. It wasn't even until they said this that it hit me: **I'm going to be a sister to this new baby!** Being a big sister will be VERY exciting, much more exciting than simply having a tiny crying baby in our home.

I agree with my *abuelos*—I think I will be a VERY good older *hermana*. Even when I am not the most patient human being on earth and even when I might not have all the answers to questions this baby might ask.

CHAPTER **8**

As camp goes on, skating has become a little easier. I no longer have to push a loud bucket around, and I've even managed to skate to the other side of the rink on my own without falling. Back at home, Lucas is learning to run by my side while I skate, which has made our sprees to the Herrera brothers' shop especially *divertidas!*

When I told the Herrera brothers that I'm going to be an older sister, they got very *felices* for me. They said I'll enjoy having a sibling. They told me that nothing makes them happier in life than having each other as *familia*. I'm not so sure they're telling the entire truth. I've seen them bicker BIG. TIME. I wonder if bickering happens with all siblings or just with the Herrera brothers. At least they agree that having a sibling is a good thing. Lucas and I thank them for the bananas they shared with us and leave them mid-bicker.

I sometimes wonder if Lucas gets offended by all these comments about siblings. For sure Lucas is more than my best *amigo*—he is my furry *hermano.* He has been there for me since I was born and hasn't left my side since. Even when I travel, or while I'm at school, I think about him and I feel **warm and happy** inside. I hope he feels the same way about me.

CHAPTER 9

Because of Mami having to stay in bed, some things at home have changed. I've been cleaning up after myself more, and Luis and I have been making breakfast together. Surprisingly, things are okay. Mami is still the best cook in the entire *mundo*, but Luis isn't half bad. He's been showing me how to chop things very carefully in order to make my favorite *repollitas* recipe, and he even let me pour the batter in the pan while making pancakes last Sunday.

I've also learned to vacuum with Mami shouting direc-
tions from her *cama*. I can't always hear what she's saying, but aside from sucking in a school report, a sock, and
part of Mami's favorite tablecloth, I think I'm doing a
pretty good *trabajo*.

Meanwhile, the baby and Mami's belly continue to grow. From time to time, I tell some stories to the hole-making *bebé*, though I find it a little silly to talk to my mami's tummy. How can this baby hear anything through Mami's belly button? It's hard to say. I tell the baby about Lucas and my love for *fútbol* and my *amigos* at school and at camp.

Every now and then, Mami's belly will move and Mami will let me feel how the baby $kicks$ and twirls. Mami says it doesn't hurt, that it just feels funny. I guess my sibling-to-be might also be a *fútbol* fan? I share a few more stories about *fútbol*.

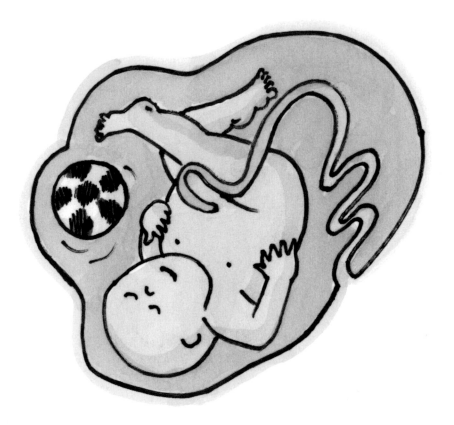

I've had to tell the baby more serious things, too, like it should STOP making holes in that sack.

Mami tells stories, too, some I'd never heard before.
Like things that happened when I was a baby (which was
a VERY long time ago!). She says that I loved sleeping and
listening to stories. I still like those things, but now I love
reading and playing with Lucas even more. Mami says
even though life will be *diferente* once this new baby is
born, all will be okay.

CHAPTER **10**

Tuesday started like any other school-break weekday. I had breakfast with Luis and then he took me to skating camp, and when camp was over, my *abuelos* picked me up. But instead of going to their *casa*, we went to the hospital. While I was at camp, Mami had been at home, and she started feeling a little funny. So Luis took her to the hospital to be sure everything was all right. She is still there, so now my *abuelos* and I are going to visit her.

Things are really quiet in the part of the hospital called the maternity ward. I haven't seen Mami yet, but my *abuelo*'s doctor friends told him that all is basically fine. It seems like the baby is ready to be born now!

After a few hours of doing crosswords with Abuelita
and sharing chocolate ice cream with Abue, I'm able to
see Mami for a couple of *minutos*.

I stand by her bed and I notice the beeping machines attached to her belly and one of her fingers. Abue says they are there to show us how well Mami's and the baby's hearts are beating.

My mami seems calm. I know she is very brave, and unlike me, she doesn't often tell anyone when she's in pain. But she assures me all is fine and gives me a big *beso*, and I believe her. She says it will be best for me to spend the night with my *abuelos*. This will be the l o n g e s t *noche* ever in the history of the whole wide world!

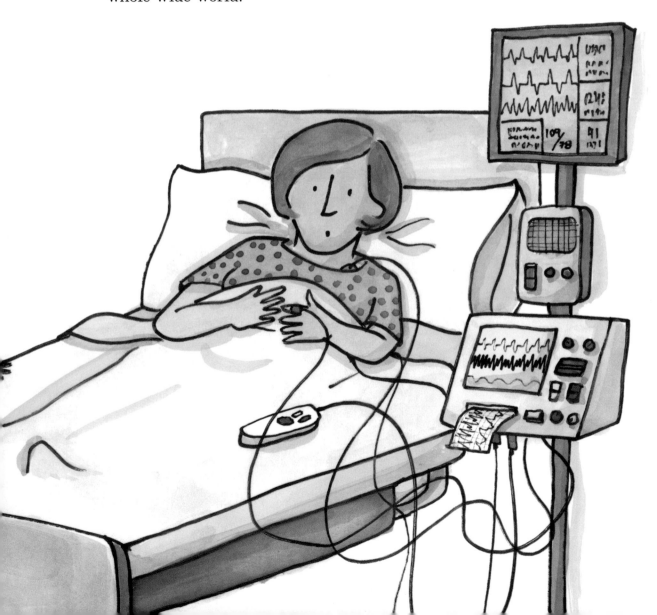

My *abuelos* take me home to pick up Lucas and to get my toothbrush and pajamas and a few changes of clothes in case I spend more than one night with them. As much as I love spending the night at Abue and Abuelita's, I hope this *bebé* comes out soon so that we can all go home together.

All the excitement from the day makes me want to talk to Lucas for *horas*. Thank goodness he is such a good listener, even with his eyes closed!

CHAPTER 11

The next morning, Abue makes me the most delicious *desayuno*. After a long shower using fancy shampoo and silky lotions, Abuelita brushes my hair and makes my pigtails look more *perfectas* than ever. Once we are ready, we drive to the hospital.

As soon as we get to the hospital, we learn that the baby was born. A sister! *Wow.*

The baby is not in Mami's arms as I'd imagined. Because she was born too small and early, she has to be in a glass box called an incubator for a while. She's the most *pequeñita* baby I've ever seen. She looks like a little pink raisin, her skin all wrinkly.

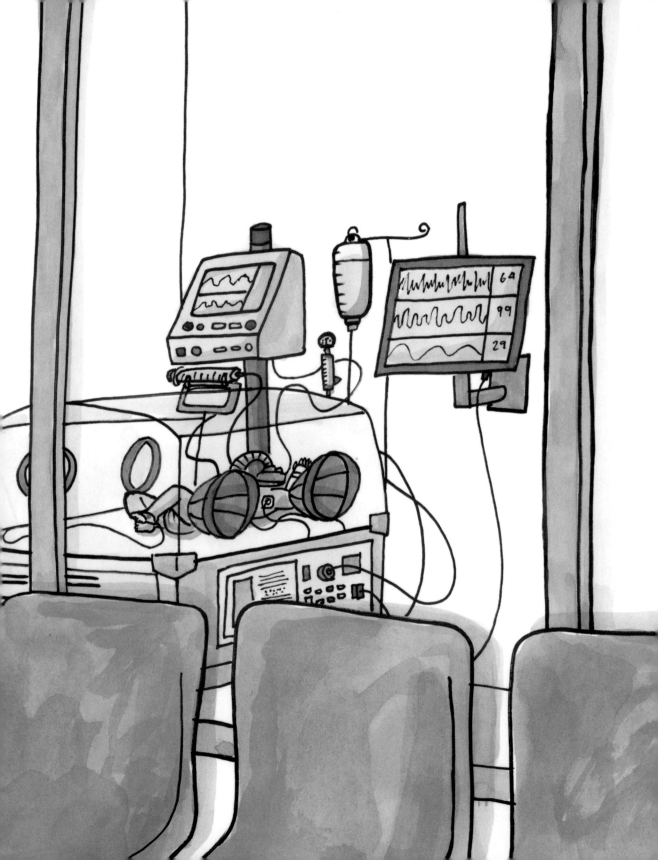

I don't go to camp today. Instead, I spend hours looking at my new baby sister through a large window.

Besides a tiny diaper, some fancy sunglasses, and a teeny hat, she's not wearing anything else. I wonder how she feels now that she isn't in Mami's belly anymore.

My *abuelos* keep me company while we wait to see Mami. Abue answers all my questions about incubators and tiny babies. He tells me that the incubator is supposed to help my sister stay warm and that all the gadgets around her are meant to keep her safe while she gains some strength. Something that looks like a tiny camera on her forehead is attached to a tube over her mouth, which helps her breathe. Then there's a very thin cable taped to her cheek and leading up into her nose. It apparently goes all the way to her tummy so she can be fed. She doesn't even know how to eat yet! There are also colorful cables keeping track of her lungs and her beating *corazón*. Abue says these cables do not hurt her, which is a big relief!

Mami tells me she is proud of me for being so patient with all of the changes that have been taking place. I'm happy to hear her say that. Mami also tells me that the new baby's name is María.

I wonder why no one asked me about names! I'm sure I could have suggested a more original *nombre* than María (so many people are called María!), but I guess I'll have to learn to call her that.

After washing my hands for what seemed like 832 *minutos*, Luis and Mami are taking me to get a closer look at María.

I want to touch my *hermanita* and hold her in my arms, but we'll have to wait for this to happen.

Mami assures me that as María gets stronger, all the cables and tubes will come off and we'll be able to hold her.

This means I will have to be even MORE patient! That won't be easy, not one bit, but as *terriblemente* hard as this is, I guess we don't have much of a choice.

I've read a book about it.

Then I went to see the Herrera brothers . . .

My chin is healing faster than I thought it would.

. . . but Abue told me it would be okay.

First I didn't like the name but then . . .

Oh, you should have seen it!

When you come home . . .

It hurt just a little bit.

I'm so excited for you!

It was unbelievable!

Mami asked if I wanted to tell María any stories while I visited. So I filled her in on all that has happened since I last spoke with her, which was while she was still in Mami's belly, in the sack with the hole. I also told her she should not tear any more holes in anything while she's at the hospital. I'm not sure that would go over too well.

Skating isn't that easy, but it isn't terribly hard . . .

. . . but I painted them all yellow and blue.

Andrea was saying I could call . . .

. . . three high jumps . . .

. . . perhaps a little uncomfortable . . .

CHAPTER 12

Because Mami and María have to stay at the hospital for a while longer, Lucas and I continue to stay with my *abuelos*. It's actually really nice to wake up at their place. From my bed, I can hear Abue humming soft tunes while he squeezes oranges for our juice. As the scent of fresh *café* takes over the whole *casa*, I come out of my room and Abuelita shares the comics section of the newspaper with me. Time at my *abuelos'* house goes by so nicely, it makes me feel a little better about having to wait SO. LONG. for Mami and María to leave the hospital.

The other thing that helps me be a little more patient is skating camp. Abue and Abuelita have made sure I always make it to Cuchavira right on time to start my warm-ups. I've shared every single little *detalle* about María with Cata, Andrea, and Camilo.

While baby María learns to breathe and eat on her own, I've been learning how to do more skating tricks. I've learned to do some loops, and once, I was even able to glide backward on my skates! I never thought I'd be able to do any of this.

Camp will be ending next week, and I will need to show all of my skating moves to Anita and Francisco in order to get a certificate. Hopefully I will do okay. I have been *practicando* as much as I can. In fact, Abuelita has asked me to please stop skating in her *casa*. So I have been pretend-training, gliding on the very smooth hallway floor wearing only my wool socks. Lucas has been incredibly helpful, volunteering to be a very strict judge while I show him all that I've learned, over and over again.

Because I have been sharing so many great things about María with them, my new *amigos* from camp are now hoping to meet this famous baby. We are all eager for her to come home. I hope it happens before camp ends!

While I wait for my baby sister to leave the hospital, I've made sure things at home are ready for her. Abuelita has driven me to our place a couple of times so we can prepare for María and Mami's arrival. While she dusts the place and sets fresh *rosas* and *magnolias* in vases, I've put my favorite *libros* in María's room and arranged the baby's teeny-tiny clothes. I've also made a few special welcome cards where I've written *muy importante* life advice for María.

This is what I want my sister to know:

Don't bother eating green beans; they taste like slimy grass.

Candy might taste *delicioso*, but if you eat too much, it will make your stomach hurt. Eating all the delicious candy in the world is not worth the pain.

Make good friends, like Lucas. Good *amigos* make everything in life a little easier.

Being kind might be hard at times, but it's worth it—like when you have some delicious cookies all for your sweet self, and want to eat all of them on your own . . . but as hard as it is, you choose to share with your friends.

Play *fútbol*. It makes your body *feliz*, even when you're feeling a little *triste*.

Life is hard—MUY. HARD.—but it gets better with practice.

CHAPTER 13

Despite being quite *nerviosa* the morning of my last day of camp, I managed to do the five short hops, I completed the three long laps around the skating rink, and I even did a high jump! All without falling a single time. Francisco and Anita were quite impressed, and I must say, my friends' loud cheers sure helped me feel confident through the whole thing.

At last, my ultra-dedicated training paid off, big time!
I got my official Skating Camp Completion Certificate, and
it even has a BIG shiny pink star!

To encourage María to get stronger faster, I've taped my shiny certificate close to her incubator. I hope it will **inspire her** to keep working as hard as I did so she can come home *muy pronto*.

Por medio de este documento
certificamos que
Juana
completó su entrenamiento
básico de patinaje

As time goes on, I've realized María's name suits her very well. It's actually a really nice name. And while she won't be able to say or spell it for a while, I'll make sure everyone knows

María is my little *hermana*.

I know my whole family will be back home soon. It will probably be quite messy at first, but with time, I'm sure we'll figure it all out. Soon enough, I'll be showing María how to kick a striking goal. I will lend her my weird skates, and we will cook new recipes together. We will make up stories no one knows yet, and we will sing old *canciones* at the top of our lungs.

It'll be **fun** to be María's big sister,

even if I have to keep on learning
to be **patient!**

Just like skating camp hasn't been all that bad, it turns out having a new baby sister isn't so terrible, either.

Perhaps it takes a second or third or fourth or even a fifth look to realize that what at first seemed awful is actually not all that bad. In fact, some things might even turn out to be really *fantásticas.*

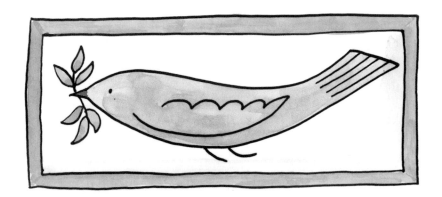

Praise for

Juana & Lucas

AN ABC BEST BOOKS FOR YOUNG READERS SELECTION
AN AMERICAN LIBRARY ASSOCIATION NOTABLE CHILDREN'S BOOK
WINNER OF A PURA BELPRÉ AUTHOR AWARD
AN INTERNATIONAL READING ASSOCIATION NOTABLE BOOK FOR A GLOBAL SOCIETY
A *HORN BOOK* FANFARE SELECTION
A *BOOKLIST* EDITORS' CHOICE
A *SCHOOL LIBRARY JOURNAL* BEST BOOK OF THE YEAR
A JUNIOR LIBRARY GUILD SELECTION

"This delightful easy chapter book has much to recommend it. . . .
Both edifying and entertaining, this solid title is a winner."
—*Bulletin of the Center for Children's Books*

"Medina's beautiful, vivid prose conjures the Colombian setting with tactile language. . . .
Juana's narration is also peppered with easy-to-figure-out Spanish words."
—*The New York Times Book Review*

★ "Fans of Judy Moody . . . will absolutely love Juana."
—*Booklist* (starred review)

★ "The stuff of true literature."
—*School Library Journal* (starred review)

★ "Will be much beloved for its warmly depicted family relationships,
eminently read-aloud-able high jinks, and sunny protagonist."
—*The Horn Book* (starred review)

Praise for

Juana & Lucas
BiG PROBLEMAS

AN ABC BEST BOOKS FOR YOUNG READERS SELECTION
A BANK STREET COLLEGE BEST CHILDREN'S BOOK OF THE YEAR
A *HORN BOOK* FANFARE SELECTION
A *SCHOOL LIBRARY JOURNAL* BEST BOOK OF THE YEAR
A JUNIOR LIBRARY GUILD SELECTION

"Medina's illustrations are a wonderful addition to Juana's
first-person narration, truly bringing her emotions and quirkiness
to life. . . . Medina's charming follow-up to her Pura Belpré
Award–winning *Juana & Lucas* doesn't disappoint."
—*Booklist*

★ "Medina's cartoon-style illustrations done in ink and watercolor
are vibrant and full of movement, beautifully capturing
the full range of Juana's conflicting emotions."
—*Kirkus Reviews* (starred review)

★ "Juana can always count on her family's steady and secure love to help solve
even the biggest problemas. The result is a thriving, buoyant, confident
young Juana who demonstrates that balancing new changes with old favorites
is achievable and, indeed, can be done with humor and grace."
—*The Horn Book* (starred review)

JUANA MEDINA was born and grew up in Bogotá, Colombia. At school, she got into trouble for drawing cartoon versions of her teachers. Eventually, however, all that drawing (and trouble) paid off. Juana Medina is the author-illustrator of *Juana & Lucas*, which won the 2017 Pura Belpré Author Award, and *Juana & Lucas: Big Problemas*. She is also the author-illustrator of the picture books *1 Big Salad*, *ABC Pasta*, and *Sweet Shapes* and the illustrator of *Smick!* by Doreen Cronin, *Lena's Shoes Are Nervous: A First-Day-of-School Dilemma* by Keith Calabrese, *I'm a Baked Potato!* by Elise Primavera, and *Star of the Party* by Jan Carr. Juana Medina lives with her family in the DC area.